A FUNNY THING HAPPENED ON THE WAY TO SCHOOL...

For Lupin
—Benjamin

Text copyright © 2015 by Davide Cali.
Illustrations copyright © 2015 by Benjamin Chaud.

Library of Congress Cataloging-in-Publication Data available.

ISBN: 978-1-4521-3168-9

Manufactured in China.

Design by Ryan Hayes.
Typeset in 1820 Modern.

10 9 8 7 6 5 4 3 2

Chronicle Books LLC
680 Second Street
San Francisco, California 94107

Chronicle Books—we see things differently.
Become part of our community at www.chroniclekids.com.

A FUNNY THING HAPPENED ON THE WAY TO SCHOOL...

Davide Cali   Benjamin Chaud

chronicle books · san francisco

Well, it's a long story ...

First, some giant ants stole my breakfast.

So I went to borrow bread from the neighbors next door.
That wasn't exactly a good idea . . .

Then, on the way to the bus stop,
I was attacked by evil ninjas.

After vanquishing them, a sea of scary
majorettes got in the way.

And *then*—out of nowhere—a massive ape appeared and
mistook the school bus for a banana.

So I hopped on my skateboard, and then was
seized by some mysterious mole people.

"So, is *that* why you're late?"

No, I easily escaped.

It's just that—right after—I suddenly shrank.

And then I became gigantic.
So I decided to take three colossal steps to school . . .

But on the second step, I returned to my regular size, and fell into a pond where I had to fight off a strange blob.

Once I got the blob off my back,
an elephant grabbed me by its trunk.

Since the elephant parade was headed in the right direction, I *still* could have made it to school on time. It's just that there was an unfortunate incident with a mouse ...

Then I ran into a little girl, who asked me
to help find her grandmother's house.

Since I never had breakfast, we stopped
for a quick bite along the way.

"So, is *that* why you're late?" No! By then I wasn't far from school at all . . .

But I couldn't help following a boy going in the
opposite direction. He was playing a magic pipe . . .

So I took a shortcut, but I must have made a wrong turn,
because I landed in an unusually large spiderweb.

Luckily, I had my universal gadget belt.

I was on my way *again* when I ran into Bigfoot,
who asked me to take his picture.

Yeti asked for one, too.

Finally out of the woods, I found myself surrounded by a
flock of sheep and a team of ducks.

It made sense to help the farmers separate them.

Then because of my champion chess skills, the president called to see if I'd help save the planet from an alien invasion.

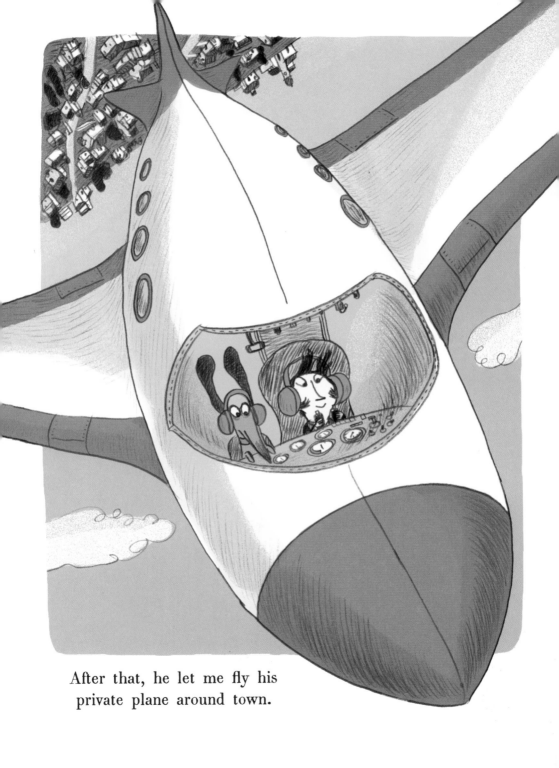

After that, he let me fly his
private plane around town.

"So, is *that* why you're late?"

Oh, no. I actually made it to school *on time*.

But I forgot my backpack . . .

So I went home to get it. Then I used my uncle's
time machine to make it back to school on time.
But something definitely went wrong . . .

And THAT is why I was late to school.

- The End -

Davide Cali is an author, illustrator, and cartoonist who has published more than 40 books, including *I Didn't Do My Homework Because* . . . He lives in Paris, France.

Benjamin Chaud has illustrated more than 60 books. He is the illustrator of *I Didn't Do My Homework Because* . . . , and the author and illustrator of New York Times Notable Book *The Bear's Song, The Bear's Sea Escape, Farewell Floppy,* as well as the Pomelo series. He lives in Die, France.